ISIS

BY GARY BOGUE

Illustrations by Carole Petersen Dwinell

Published by Lesher Communications, Inc.

Walnut Creek, California

If you have ever owned a cat, you will understand why I wrote these tales. That's also why this book is dedicated to you. Because we both know every single word between these covers is true.

ISIS
Copyright ©1990 by Lesher Communications, Inc.
All rights reserved. No part of this book may be reproduced
in any form without written permission from the publisher.

Printed in the United States of America
ISBN 0-9623012-1-3

Published by Lesher Communications, Inc.
2640 Shadelands Drive, Walnut Creek, CA 94598

Printed by Dharma Enterprises
1241 21st Street, Oakland, CA 94607

Illustrations: Carole Petersen Dwinell
Photo: Jon McNally
Design: Patricia Brinton
Composition: Terri Markey

Forward

Isis is a real cat.

It's hard to believe it, I know, but life is like that.

It seems like only yesterday when she first stormed into my life. Ah yes, it was a dark and stormy night, and a knock came at my door. I'm sure you've heard this ugly tale before.

After carefully fastening the chainlock, I eased open the door to see who was there. That was my first mistake. Whoever heard of a cat paying attention to a chainlock?

My second mistake was in stepping outside to look around. She slammed the door behind me and locked me out in the rain.

When I finally broke a window to let myself back in, she wouldn't even get me a towel.

She has allowed me to sleep in the spare bedroom ever since.

Now do you believe she's real?

I thought you might.

Gary Bogue

Meet my new cat

It's so cold in my house I had to send my brass monkey over to stay with friends.

If you don't know anything about brass monkeys, that means it's VERY cold.

You're going to ask me what this has to do with my new cat, aren't you? Since you asked …

My house is supposed to be heated with a little jim-dandy Sears Wall Heater. I said "supposed" to be heated because it isn't. Heated, I mean. I mean the wall heater. I mean I don't turn it on. I mean I can't turn it on. Oh heck, this is really embarrassing.

Mycatwon'tletmeturnonthedarnheater!

I know this sounds stupid, but you have to understand that "Isis" (after an Egyptian nature goddess I used to date in my youth) is a Siamese cat. No … she's a SIAMESE! cat. That's a specially prepared hybrid mixture of blue point/red point/seal point—in her case all the *worst* points—Siamese cat breeds all smooshed into one gorgeous and *powerful* hunk of fine-tuned feline fastidiousness. With blue eyes, salt and pepper smokey-flavored body, black tail and feet. And bright orange ears.

And when Isis MERRROWWS! … everybody listens.

Especially me.

Like when I get home from work, walk into my front room freezer and turn on the little jim-dandy Sears' Wall Heater. A loud little fan turns on to blow hot air into the room and scares Isis to death and makes her MERRROWW. And that vocal laser beam instantly penetrates my normally protective headbones and congeals my brain into imitation banana pudding.

And if I don't immediately kill the Monster With The Hot Breath, Isis stalks across the room, raises my pant leg, lowers my sock top, takes a firm grip with all four feet ... and turns the soft area between ankle and knee into a shredded stump of used corncob.

That's why I keep the goosedown comforter folded up on the end of the couch. To wrap up the frozen carcass. *My* frozen carcass.

Yesterday morning I knew something finally had to be done.

I picked myself up from where I had plowed into the dining room table after sliding across the kitchen ice rink, stalked across the living room to the little jim-dandy Sears Wall Heater, tripped over the coffee table because I'd forgotten to turn on the lights, flipped on the Monster With The Hot Breath ... and dashed back across the dining room, slid on my chin across the kitchen ice rink and through the door on the other side, plowed into the toilet bowl and knocked all the breath out of my body, but still managed to reach up and lock myself in the bathroom with my toe.

The next few minutes were some of the most frightening moments of my life. The beast raged outside the bathroom door and threw its enormous body against the wood again and again until it shuddered so violently from the blows that I feared for my very life.

And then it got deathly quiet.

And then the doorknob turned slowly to the left, and slowly to the right.

Thank God I had locked it!

And then all was still again.

After half an hour of utter silence, I slowly opened the door and peered out. There was nothing in sight. No sound to be heard but the heavy panting of the Monster With The Hot Breath. I began to get concerned.

After a 15 minute search, I knew the worst. Isis was gone.

I sat down on the couch (well, after all I'd just been through, why shouldn't I enjoy the warmth?) and thought about it. And the more I thought about it the better it started to sound. Good Lord ... I was free!

I glanced down to discover the radiant Isis, who was stretched languorously beneath the little jim-dandy Sears Wall Heater, lazily flicking the end of her tail as she soaked up the warmth.

Shaking my head in amazement at the fickleness of female felines, I took my shower and got ready for work. On the way out, I stopped to turn off the little jim-dandy Sears Wall Heater.

Isis opened one deadly blue eye and growled.

I think we've got a problem here ...

Cloud Nine Lives

I think I just made a misteak.

I made one once before it was around 1954 if my memory serves me. Two misteaks in 30 years. Geeze, I must be slipping.

I was at the supermarket loading up with my weekly supply of TV dinners when I happened to take a shortcut down the aisle where they stocked the pet supplies. That's where I discovered they were having a sale on catnip.

That's also where I made my misteak.

I bought some.

And I took it home.

Isis was snoring softly on the back of the couch. She'd been up late the night before watching Return of the Cat People on the late-late-show.

She was on remote control and one orange ear cocked sharply in my direction to make sure I belonged, and then snapped back in acknowledgement. I sighed softly and my hands stopped shaking when I saw I'd passed inspection. First time this week.

Isis is better than any radar security system on the market. She has a special mode called "Overkill." If there's any question she automatically attacks. Normal people might call that a drawback, but I really don't care to discuss it any further. It makes my ankles hurt just thinking about it.

I quietly opened the catnip and sprinkled some on the rug by the front door, then stood back to watch. I wasn't sure quite what to expect.

For about 30 seconds, all was normal ... then ...

SPRONG! Two vivid blue sapphires suddenly bulged from the sockets that used to hold her eyes and the room abruptly tipped sideways, caught in the turbulent backwash from a rolling cacophony of uncontrollably seductive purrs.

Isis poured down the back of the couch like hot maple syrup out of a saucepan ... dripped onto the floor ... gurgled across the room to the front door ... and started soaking into the rug where I'd sprinkled the catnip.

All I could see was the orange tips of her ears, drunkenly cruising through the shag piling like a shark prowling around a freshly sunken wine tanker.

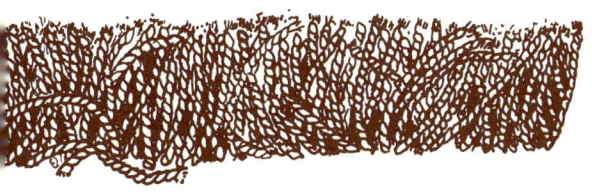

That was the first time. It was slightly different the second. None of that sensuous, laid-back, melt into the rug and dream away the rest of the afternoon scene.

The second time she simply went berserk.

It was kind of interesting, in a surrealistic sort of way, looking down from where I was hanging onto the brass light fixture in my dining room ceiling. Ever since I was a kid I've always wondered what it would be like to bring a power-mower into the house.

I was getting kind of tired of that long shag, anyway.

The next morning, while Isis was still sleeping it off, I sealed the rest of the catnip inside every plastic bag I had left in the house and stashed it in the safest, most airtight place I could think of. Then, shaking my head ruefully and taking one last glance at Isis, where she was still draped over the top of the swag lamp in the corner, I headed for work.

That night, Isis wasn't at the door to greet me as she usually does. I found the first signs of impending disaster in my office. All my desk drawers were open and papers were strewn carelesly on the floor as if ... someone were looking for something ...

I ran for the kitchen, my thoughts racing frantically ahead. The icebox door was open ... and so was the freezer! She found it! Oh no, not a whole bag of the stuff!

I roamed the house, calling her, pleading ... checking the microwave to see if she was sleeping it off ... her secret hiding place behind my cowboy boots. But she was nowhere to be found.

And then I saw it—hanging in mid-air just above my waterbed. It was a wide, Cheshire Cat grin ... which was all that still remained after the rest of her had gone.

Living the Tweet Life

I never had a cat come when I whistled before.

I do now.

And I always seem to find these things out the hard way.

The other morning I'm strolling around the kitchen, resplendent in my bare earlymorningness, scraping my toast into the sink and generally feeling pretty good about the fact that it's Friday, and I get this sudden urge to burst forth in whistle.

Wheet! Wheet! de wheedle wheet ... in Dixie!

And that's when I discovered that my she-beast, Isis, fearsome orange-eared goddess of all she surveys—answers to a whistle. I discovered that right after I developed the limp. The limp was because Isis was wrapped around my raw right ankle, carefully licking my big toe and getting it all slicked up for the kill.

That's when I realized, in mid-stream, that Isis was strangely affected by my whistling.

My screams have a strange effect on her too. They make her purr.

After I've showered and bandaged my ankle and dressed, I decide to experiment with this new-found feline phenomenon.

I get down on my hands and knees behind the couch and peer carefully around the end. Isis is in the bedroom and I can see where she'll have to come through the kitchen into the living room. I protect my face with my hands and give a whistle.

Powheet.

Nothing happens. Interesting. Maybe the whole thing was a fluke.

OUCH!

That's when I discover that Isis wasn't in the bedroom after all.

OUCH!

That's when I discover there's another end to the couch. An unprotected end.

OUCH!

That's also when I discover there's also another end to my body. MY unprotected end.

No wonder there's such a call for new scientists in this country. Research is hell.

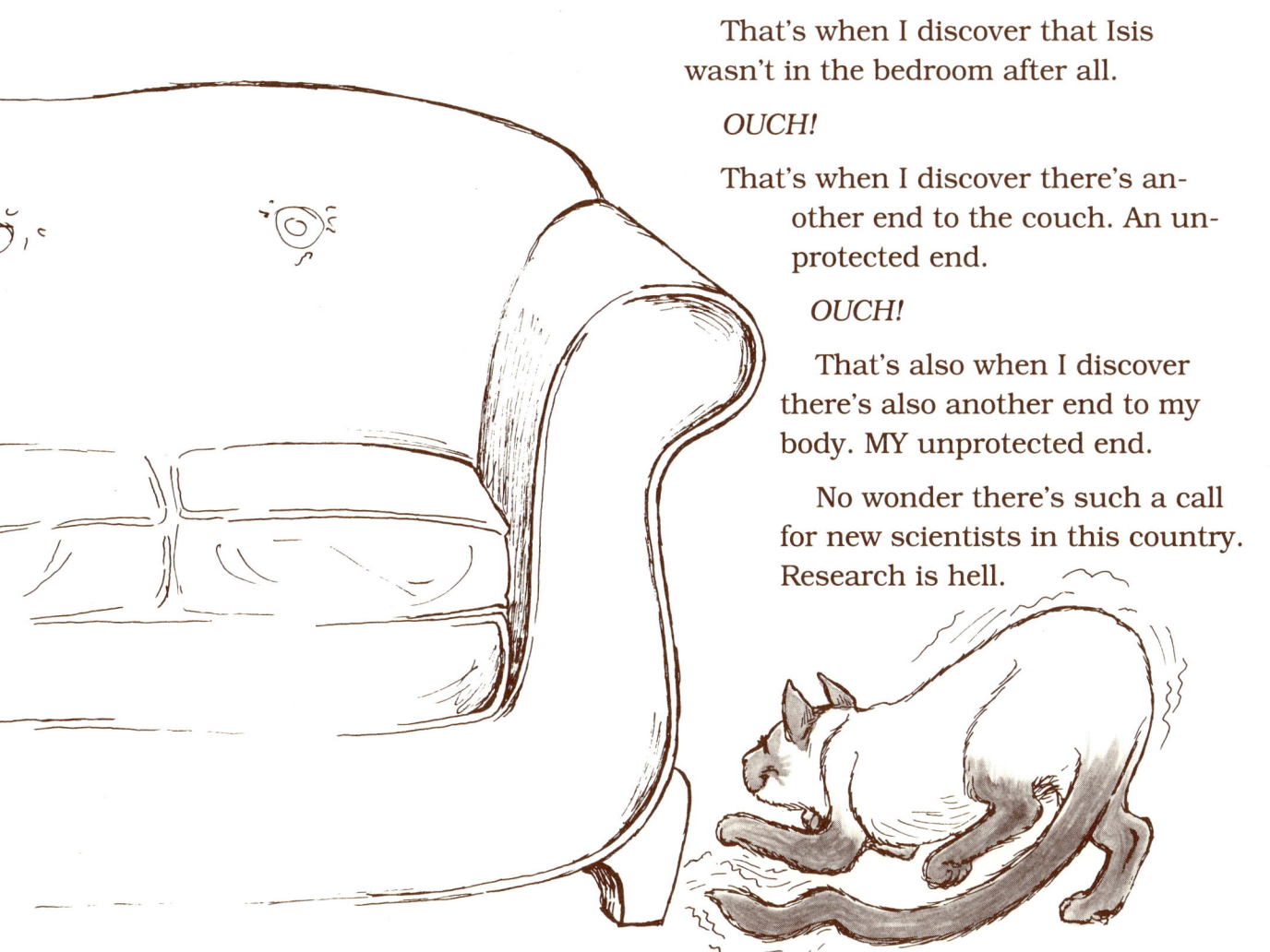

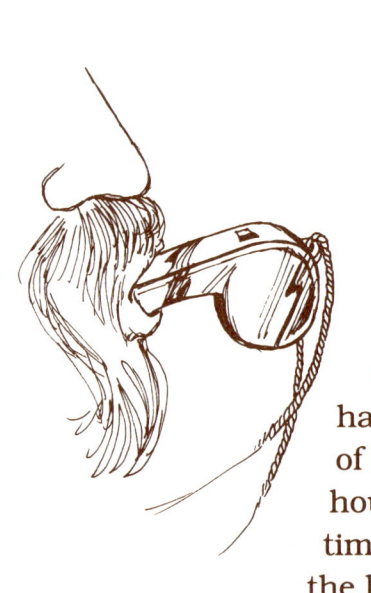

Obviously I had lost control of my own household. It was time to head for the local newspaper where I work and defuse the situation. I could hear her purrs following me all the way out to the car.

By mid-morning I had run out of ways to explain to the other columnists why I was standing up while I typed my column into the computer.

"Do you always stand on your left foot like that?" twittered our gossip columnist. "You look like a bird."

On the way home after I picked up my TV dinner at the supermarket, I made a side stop at the hardware store. No cat was going to kick ME around in my own house! No way! If a pet columnist can't deal with his own pet problems, who will?

I will, replied the inner me, with my shiny new chrome-plated police whistle with the bright red nylon cord!

I sat down on the couch, crossed my legs and smiled. I puckered up my lips and made ready to whistle.

Isis tensed her waiting body, got a good grip with her front paws on the top shelf of the bookcase and braced her back feet against the ceiling ...

Pweet!

She launched herself gloriously into the air —to splatter against the solid wall of sound that issued from my shiny new police whistle.

"Now we'll see who gets the last laugh THIS time," I smiled down at the quivering pool of orange and blue Jell-o at my feet, gently twirling my shiny new police whistle on the end of its bright red nylon cord.

BAT! A paw appeared from the pool to take a swipe at the whistle. BAT!

'That's more like it," I laugh. "Start acting like a normal little kitty and stop acting like you own the place." I dropped the whistle on the rug and went to stick my TV dinner in the microwave.

On the way to bed I spotted the end of the bright red nylon cord. She'd buried my shiny new police whistle in the cat box. Yuk!

Her blue eyes gleamed from the top of my pillow.

It seemed like as good a night as any to sleep on the couch.

The Grass Monster

To understand today's column, you will also have to understand that my Siamese werecat is an indoor werecat. (Though when the moon is full methinks her ruthless spirit stalks the foggy moors of the local dump.)

Bermuda grass is a notably hardy breed. It's the kind of grass a man can respect.

Unlike most grasses that just stand there and let you mow them down, blade after blade, Bermuda grass will fight back. I had a neighbor who tripped on a tough strand of the stuff and slid under his powermower and cut off the end of his boot. It missed his toes, but he sat there sobbing quietly in the middle of his lawn, cradling his foot for an hour before he got up enough nerve to check.

He was so unnerved by the whole thing that he traded his mower to the guy across the street for a six-pack of beer and hasn't touched his lawn since.

As I said, that Bermuda grass really knows how to survive.

All this passed through my mind when I first spotted the green strands growing out from under my bookcase. My front lawn had found a crack in my front wall and was trying to move into my front room!

I was initially tempted to yank the insolent intruder out by its miserable little root hairs. But then, mindful of my neighbor's missing

boot-tip, I figured, what the heck, these days people pay a fortune for exotic potted plants. If I have one that wants to move in and live with me for free — who am I to argue with fate?

So for weeks I let it grow and slowly creep up the wall behind the bookcase, and I occasionally draped it artfully over a section of unused books. I'm a sci-fi freak, so if my wild houseplant decides to languish across "Middlemarch," "Bleakhouse," or "Lox-finger," or the "Achievements of Samuel Johnson," who cares?

All well and good.

Until Isis discovered the Grass Monster.

I remember it crystal clearly. It was last Sunday at 1:37 p.m. It was a beautiful sunny day and I had all the windows and doors open and that's when a rather robust little breath of wind decided to stir up my household. Among the things that got stirred was a snakelike strand of Bermuda grass that was snoozing on the middle level of my bookcase.

SHAZAM!

G* R* A* S* S   M* O* N* S* T* E* R !

I looked up from where I was reading, a bit startled myself at the green thing that was lashing about the bookcase. I distinctly remember thinking it looked like it was growing out of the back of a copy of Frank Herbert's science fiction "Dune" trilogy, and wondering to myself if maybe I shouldn't change my reading habits.

Meanwhile, Isis glared down from where she was clinging to the ceiling.

Next thing I know she's down on her belly between me and the bookcase, a husky growl in her throat ... stalking the ugly green alien thing that has invaded our world. She gives me a quick glance over her shoulder and a high-pitched MMEow of reassurance, then turns back to protect me from the quivering tentacle ... and attacks!

BitingANDspittingANDgrowling ...

ANDclawingANDhissing!

And then silence.

I sat stunned on the couch, shocked by the explosiveness of what had just happened. Isis was behind me, peering out under my right arm. I could feel the growl still rumbling inside her belly.

Across the room the now dead blade of Bermuda grass was limp and still.

With Isis pressed tensely against my leg, alert for any movement, I got a long stick and carefully lifted the deadly thing and threw it over to the dogs in the yard next door.

Then I went back in the house to hug my brave little Isis.

That fetching Look

Teaching my screwy Siamese how to play "fetch" may have been a big mistake. Now that she's learned how, she doesn't want to stop.

The game starts when I toss a crumpled up ball of crisp paper across the room. She gets high on the crinkly sound it makes when she bats it around. After eight or 10 moves that would make a world-class soccer player drool all over his shorts, she daintily picks up the wad of paper in her mouth and trots over to drop it into my outstretched hand for another toss.

It's been weeks, now, and so far the game hasn't ended. It's the top of the 33rd inning and this pitcher is exhausted.

Everywhere I go she follows me around with that infernal ball of paper in her mouth. When a Siamese cat MERRROOOWERS it sounds bad enough, but when Isis threatens me with her mouth full it sounds like somebody stepped on the tail of a duckbill platypus.

Everytime I stop moving she drops the ball and bites me on the ankle until I play.

When I get home from work she's waiting by the door.

In the middle of the night I am awakened by an earful of crinkle as she drops it on my pillow and takes my nose gently into her mouth.

Desperately, I fight back.

I flush the paper ball. And when I turn and reach down to pet her she drops another into my hand.

Cleverly, I modify the game by flipping the wad up onto the top shelf of my floor-to-ceiling bookcase.

Politely she refrains from handing me the ball until I've finished picking up the books.

Over the years I've taught a lot of different animals to play fetch but never has one become as obsessed with doing this awful thing as Isis has.

I once raised an arctic wolf that desperately wanted to be a good fetcher. He would charge madly across the yard after the big softball, bowling over anything that dared to cross his path (boulders, trees), his great mouth open in a happy grin and his awesome tongue flapping in the wind. He only had one problem, but it was big enough to keep him from getting signed by the 49ers. He always ate the ball before he got it back to me.

And there was this young mountain lion that was relentless in her eagerness to please. When we'd go exploring on Mount Diablo, I'd toss balls into nearby thickets and she'd leap gracefully from sight. I lost a lot of balls with that big cat. She always brought back a rabbit or a squirrel. But never any balls.

Even Khyber, my old 10-foot Burmese python, took a random bank-shot at playing fetch with me and some rubber beach balls. It still gives me a chuckle whenever I think about that sunny afternoon by the pool. He looked like he had a case of the lumps as he bobbed happily along on the surface of the water. I always liked to take Khyber with me when I went to public pools. That way it was never too crowded.

Yes, I've played fetch with wolf, lion and python, but none of them ever threatened to kill me if I quit.

It takes the warped mind of a female Siamese cat named Isis to come up with an idea like that.

OK, we're talking desperate here if you know what I mean and I think you do. How do I get my fur-lined roommate to end this crazy stupid game?

Excuse me now, but I have to go.

My ankles are killing me.

off the walls

It was a dark and stormy night, and a knock came at my door.

I lay there in the blackness, not sure what had awakened me, my muscles tight and ready for instant action. Columnists need good reflexes if they plan to survive long in this business.

And then it came again ...

Thunk! Thunk! Thunk!

The sound of a huge wet fist from out of the raging wind and fearsome torrents of rain that fought around my lonely cottage walls that night.

I slid from under the covers in one smooth motion, even as the hackles were rising on the back of my neck. I eased low out the bedroom door and across the kitchen and poked my head cautiously around the side of my video arcade Battlezone game. But it was too dark to see anything and the only sound was the sharp splatter of rain against the windows.

Thunk!

It came again. Only ... this ... time ... from inside my front room!

OK, now, we're talking heavy duty fear here! Another surge of adrenalin like that and I'll have to skip my morning coffee for the next month. I flipped on the lights just as there was another

Thunk!

I peeked around the Battlezone game again, I don't know, expecting maybe the bride of Frankenstein, or at the very least a dark and fearsome stranger. Certainly not my stupid Siamese who was kicking books off the top shelf of my floor-to-ceiling bookcase.

"Oh ... you're gonna die for this one, you ... "

I stalked across the room and reached up for her, only instead of a mew I got the loud, mournful *Yeowl* of a terrified cat and three more *Thunk! Thunk! Thunks!* as she tried to burrow deeper behind the dwindling rows of books.

Hummmm.

"OK, what's the problem here?" I said, trying a new tack. "You got me up, now what do you want me to do?"

"It wants to get me!" she *Yeowled*, kicking off the last of my collection of Isaac Asimov and starting in on poor old Ray Bradbury.

"Where? I don't see anything," I answered, wondering if I should go stand on a table.

"Under the bookcase!" she *Yeowled*. *"It's back!"*

"Oh no," I thought. "Not that."

But when I snapped on the table lamp and tilted the shade and bent low to look, I could see the rays glinting off those familiar pus-green coils. The Grass Monster had returned!

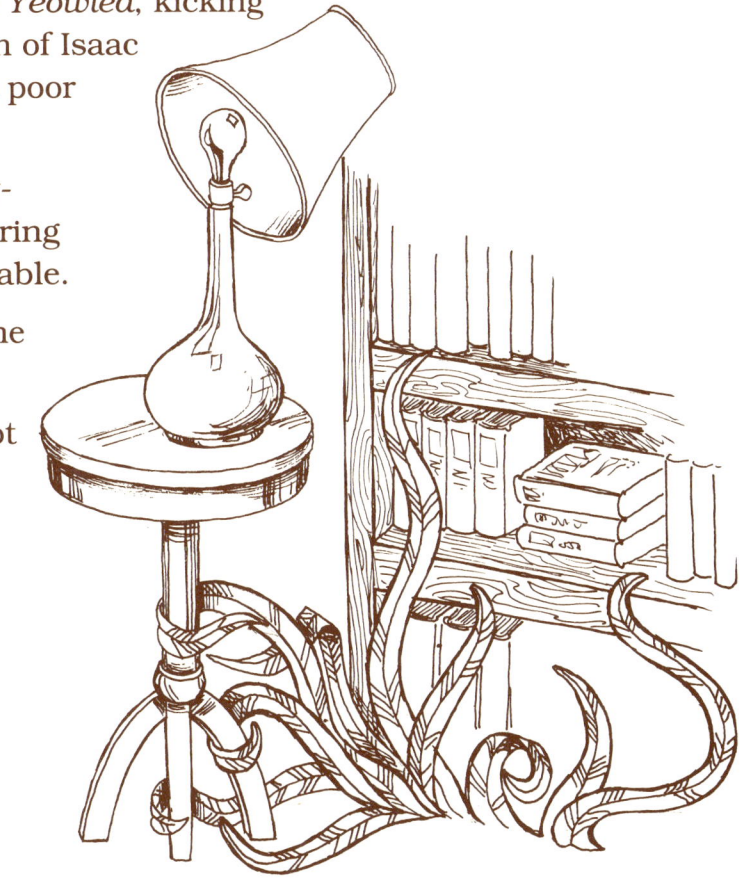

The scourge of indoor cats everywhere, the Grass Monster lurks deep beneath my lawn, waiting its chance to push up through that secret crack in the wall beneath my bookcase—its only known link to the outside world—and ensnare my dear Isis in its loathsome, jointed, Kryptonite-green tentacles.

"Stand back!" I shouted. "It's the Grass Monster!"

The *Yeowling* got louder.

"Not MY cat, you, you scourge!" I demanded. "You'll have to take ME first!"

The *Yeowling* stopped.

I lunged across the living room and snatched the giant long-handled stainless steel hedge clippers from their sheath in the hall closet.

"Stand back, Isis," I smiled grimly, springing lightly to my toes. "It's all mine."

The ensuing battle was much too gory to recount here. Suffice it to say the satisfying snicks of my trusty blades left no doubt as to the eventual winner.

I threw the last of those limp dead coils out the door and turned to my faire Isis.

"Tis done, m'lady, the monster is no more!"

Her loud purrs as she rubbed gratefully against my leg were more than ample reward for this knight's deed.

I know, I know, it's a wacky little household, but somebody's got to live here.

Convivial Pursuit

Well, it's the last day of Super Bowl Week and while you're out there cracking that first beer and reaching for a potato chip and waiting for the big game to start, I want you to know I'm sitting here hunched up on the couch in front of my TV set and fearing for my very life.

Possibly you could find it in your heart to say a small prayer just before kickoff.

I have a problem. It's Isis. My schizophrenic Siamese supercat.

She's become a football freak.

Last week she started reading our sports columnist's daily diatribes about The Game and as each day passed my frantic feline got more and more caught up in the excitement and frenzy that was being generated by my locker room associates at the paper.

It started out with little things, at first.

On Monday she wouldn't give me the sports section. No biggie. I could always get another at the office.

On Tuesday she finally agreed to let me have the sports section but told me not to come home unless I brought it back with our sports columnist's autograph on his picture. Now THAT hurt. She'd never asked me for mine. I could see that getting through the rest of the week maybe wasn't going to be as easy as I first thought.

Wednesday I arrived home to discover she'd gathered up all her crumpled paper balls and piled them on the coffee table so we could do a little passing and running practice. That was actually kind of fun until she missed the ball and bit my typing finger on a Statue of Liberty play.

Thursday when I got home from work, I discovered she'd gathered up all her paper balls again, dyed them brown and was drop-kicking them through the portable antenna on top of my TV set. That was OK, I guess, but by bedtime I was exhausted from fetching them back for her from the windowsill.

On Friday, for the first time since I've known her, Isis had an accident during her morning constitutional. Fortunately I always spread newspapers under her cat box. On this occasion I noticed it happened to be the sports section. It was open to a story about the Miami Dolphins with a large color picture of coach Don Shula.

Sorry, coach.

When I awoke on Saturday morning she blind-sided me on the way to the showers.

As she stood there grinning down at me through her face mask, I knew I was in deep trouble. During the night my gentle Isis had undergone a startling metamorphosis and emerged in the dawn to become one of the most fearsome creatures known to inhabit the earth this time of year.

A San Francisco 49er fan!

As I lay there gasping and trying to catch my breath, she pulled off her shiny red and gold helmet, spit out the rubber mouthpiece and started to purrrrrr.

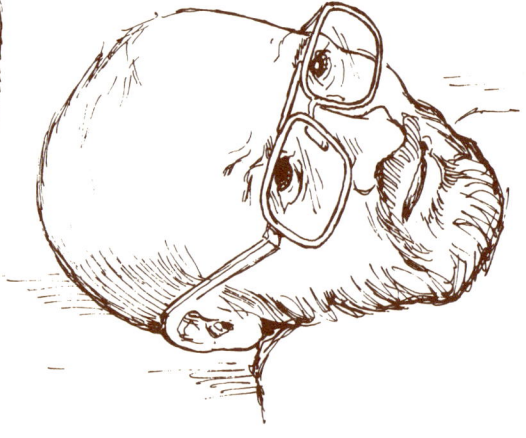

So here it is. Super Bowl Sunday.

The day every sports fan in the world but me has been waiting for.

Today when I got up to fix coffee I found my only clean sheet hanging from the bookcase. Large red letters spelled out: *Nuke The Dolphins!*

My hand started to shake as I plugged in the coffeepot.

And now I'm sitting here, waiting for the game to start and, as I said at the beginning of this suicide note, fearing for my life.

You see, there is an enormous black panther stretched clear across the back of the couch. One thick foreleg is hanging down and the great paw is resting heavily on my shoulder.

My Isis has a very vivid imagination.

Unfortunately so have I. That's what has me worried.

You see, I promised her the 49ers would win.

The Purrfect Solution

I have always dreaded that this day might come and now it has and I fear the world is no longer a safe place to live.

Isis, my facetious feline, has discovered the practical joke.

She started out simple. The old "bare foot in the cat puddle on the kitchen floor" joke. Very funny. And she'd diabolically refined this oldie but goodie. When I sat down to dry my foot off with a paper towel I sat down in another one. Good thing her water dish had run dry at that point or I might have drowned.

There's nothing worse than a Siamese with a sick sense of humor.

For the next week or so I relived the complete and unabridged history of the practical joke. Mouse traps in my shoes. Rubber snakes in my breakfast cereal. (Have you ever seen a cat laugh so hard it fell off a table?)

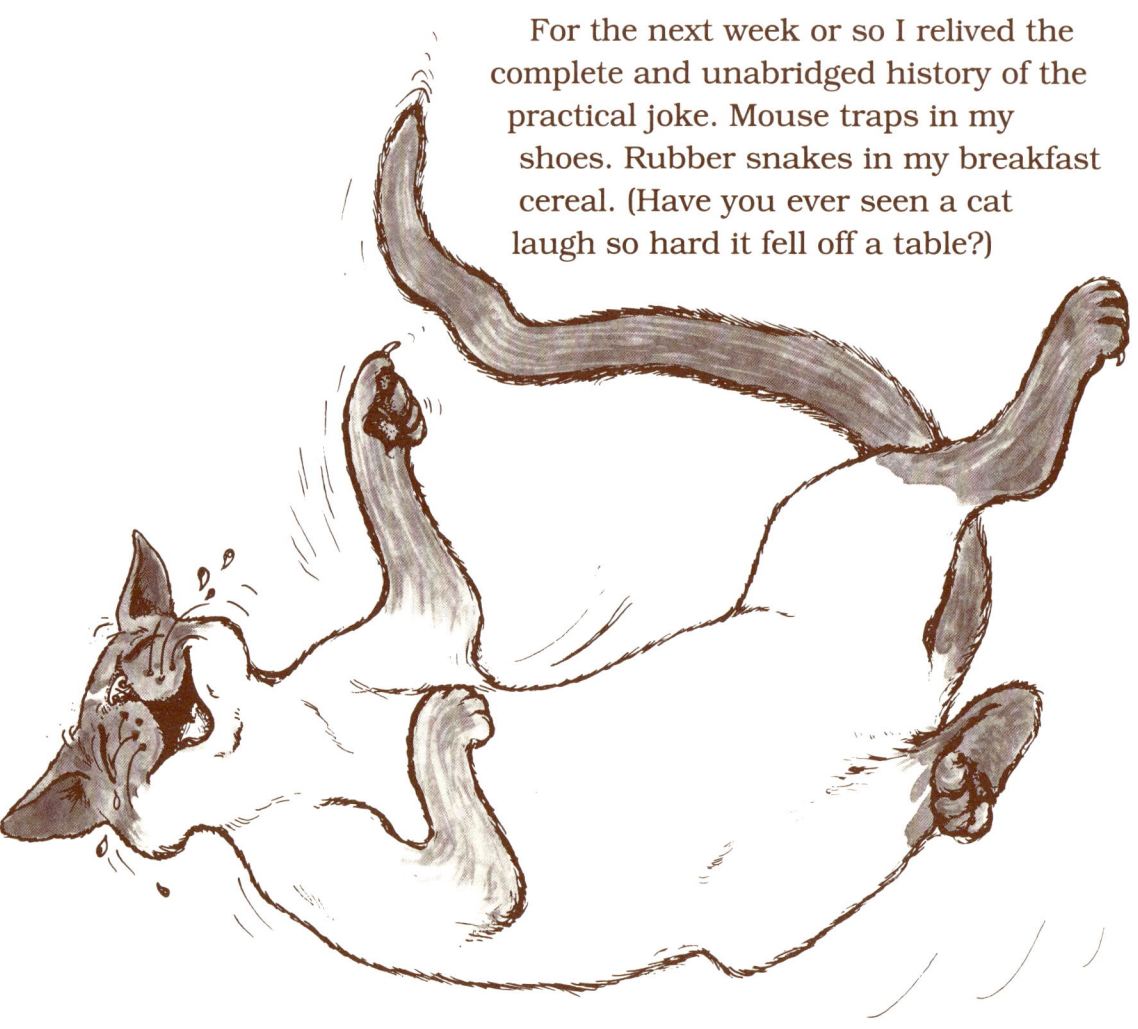

Green food coloring in my orange juice.

Whoopie cushions under my bed pillow.

And then she started to get creative.

How does one describe how it feels to step out of bed into three feet of warm shaving cream?

Or to hang up a telephone after the earpiece has been painted with superglue?

Of course you understand, this meant war.

So I buried an enema tube in her food dish and hid around the corner with a giant syringe full of ice water.

And she countered by filling my waterbed with half-frozen lime Jell-o.

So I sprinkled alum in her water dish.

Mere survival started to get tough.

It got so bad we'd lie in bed in the morning, each afraid to move until the other got up.

I missed two whole days of work.

Both of us watched television for 48 hours straight one weekend waiting for the other one to go to bed first.

Something had to be done. I couldn't take it. Our relationship was in jeopardy. We'd both stopped talking. Isis had come up with three new kinks in her tail and one whisker had developed an alarming twitch. My beard developed kinks.

I decided the only way to resolve the situation was to catch Isis with a practical joke of my own that was so shocking ... so incredibly stunning in its magnitude ... that it would cure her, once and for all, of her fiendish practical joking habits.

Quietly I began to gather together the ingredients. One super-deluxe battery-powered Ghetto Blaster dolby stereo laser disc player. A high fidelity laser disc recording of the San Francisco Zoo Lion House at feeding time. A giant three-foot-long stuffed opossum that could easily have made the Guiness Book of Records as the largest rat in the world.

One evening while Isis was watching old M*A*S*H reruns in the living room, I arranged my little drama artfully in the middle of the kitchen floor. Then I opened a brand new box of dry cat food and dumped it loudly into her empty plastic dish.

Here kitty! Isis ... DINNER!

She was still hanging from the light fixture in the dining room when I left for work the next morning.

I giggled happily all the way out to my car. The sun was just ready to clear the horizon and there was just light enough to see it was going to be a simply wonderful day.

Until I opened my car door.

My terrified scream echoed across the foothills like the startled cry of a goosed mastodon.

There was a live gorilla seated behind my steering wheel.

An Easter Surprise

Oh boy, oh boy, oh boy! It's Easter!

I probably should explain all my excitement.

You see, I've discovered that Isis has been secretly preparing an Easter "surprise" for me all week. While I've been at work, she's been at home coloring eggs. She doesn't think I know about it but I'm not so dumb. I've seen the clues.

For example, there's the 20 extra egg cartons hidden in back of the refrigerator behind all her tofu desserts. And of course the bright chartreuse and electric-blue and orange and red stains in my once-white kitchen sink. Little things like that.

I think she's really been looking forward to today. I already spotted the new Easter bonnet in the top of her closet and I know she snuck out Friday morning and had her hair done by Kathryn at Orinda Grooming. Kathryn called me at work to get an OK on her using my BankAmerica card.

Last night was the clincher. I woke up around 2 a.m. and could hear funny clanking sounds coming from the living room. I knew it! I was right! That little Easter honey was hiding all those eggs to surprise me!

When I got up this morning I felt like I was a little kid all over again. I hoped she'd taken her time and really hidden the eggs. I didn't want it to be too easy. That wouldn't be any fun.

I should worry so hard.

Well, I'll just check over here under the couch pillows … nope, too easy. Hummm. In the barrel of our antique muzzle-loading Civil War cannon lamp? Nope, nothing but spider webs. This is getting interesting. I wouldn't think there are that many places in my living room to hide 20 dozen Extra Large Grade AA eggs without at least a few of them being obvious.

Look at her perched up there on top of the suit of armor with that smug look on her face and that funny little Easter bonnet cocked over her left ear. Amazing what they can do with calla lilies these days.

Well, it's two hours later, folks, and my little straw basket is still empty.

I've combed this house from front to rear and back again. Nothing! This is getting serious. I mean, I really looked! I even climbed halfway up our potted redwood and checked the tree-house. Nothing!

A half-hour ago Isis got to laughing so hard she fell off the suit of armor and nearly impaled herself on the pike. Now she's lying on her back in the middle of the rug, giggling hysterically.

It's humiliating to be taken like this by a Siamese.

Well, I'm as good a sport as the next guy. And I can (choke) take a joke.

It's a good thing those eggs are hard-boiled. With the kind of hot weather we've been having lately, 240 raw eggs could do really rotten things to the air quality of a small house.

They are hard-boiled, aren't they? Isis?

I think you better stop laughing and answer me.

EDITOR'S NOTE IN A LOCAL NEWSPAPER: Columnist Gary Bogue appears in the Times every Saturday, Sunday, Tuesday and Thursday. Until further notice he will also be LIVING at the Times and showering with the pressmen. Friends of Isis may reach her at the newspaper's photo lab where she stashes her frozen tofu desserts in the fridge behind the lab's color film supply. Rumor has it that a small cottage in Martinez, and possibly an entire city block, may have to be evacuated by the end of the week.

A fallen angel

After a long day at work, there's no greater pick-me-up than to walk around the corner of the house and bump into a heady lungful of cool wisteria blossoms that's been waiting all day for me in the shade.

It puts me in the proper mood for dealing with my frolicsome feline, Isis, and her new game. Slightly euphoric — which is the only way to be when you deal with that scrofulous Siamese and a new game.

I have this little angel Christmas ornament ... no ... Isis has this little angel Christmas ornament. It's handmade out of what looks to be the side of one of those plastic strawberry cartons, with colored yarn woven through it in a needlepoint design (the neighborhood kids know a soft touch when it comes to raising money during the holiday season).

This little blonde angel with the white wings is a favorite of Isis'. I guess because the plastic latticework feels good in her teeth and the light softness of the yarn is so imminently battable about the room.

I know she's spent a good part of every day playing with it for months.

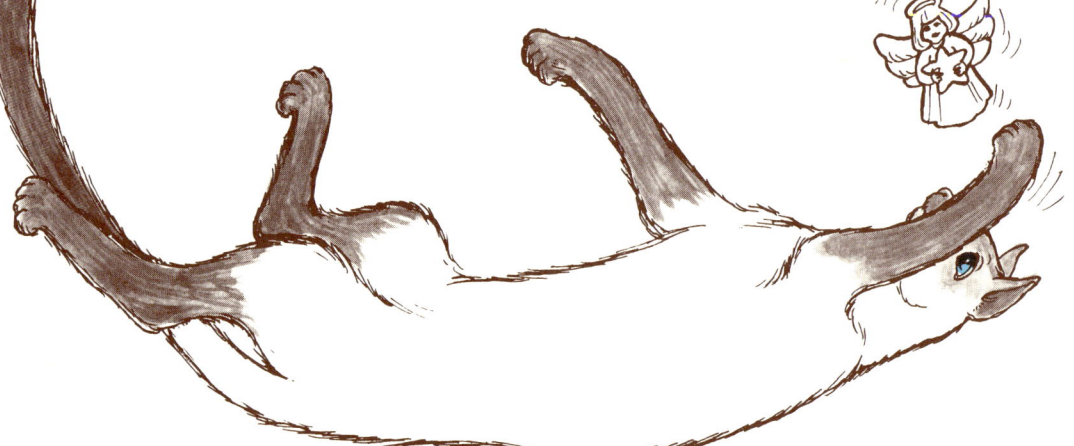

One morning, I was feeling a bit devilish, and maybe just a tad vengeful after falling prey to one of her practical jokes the night before (I thought short-sheeting went out with World War II!). On the way out the door I picked up her angel and flipped it up on the top shelf of my floor-to-ceiling bookcase when she wasn't looking.

That'll fix her little red wagon.

That night when I got home, the angel was lying quietly just inside the front door.

I looked up to find Isis staring back at me in mild amusement from the top of the stereo, where she was listening to my Beethoven tapes.

I looked back down at the angel, lying at my feet like a medieval battle gauntlet, tossed down in a challenge to the death. (That cat sure has a flare for the dramatic!)

LET THE GAMES BEGIN!

The next morning I waited until Isis was putting on her face in the bathroom before I hid the angel. I tucked it deep within the protective arms of Fang, my man-eating houseplant that hangs beside the bookcase. There was no way she was going to see her little angel in the depths of that horny mass of pulsating thorn-tipped leaves. And if, by some lucky chance she did, well ... so I skip Fang's midnight feedings for a couple of weeks.

The angel was waiting just inside the door when I got home.

A snickering Siamese is not a very pretty sight. It was plain to see I was definitely facing a challenge of monumental proportions. Fang was also facing bologna sandwiches for the rest of the month.

The next morning I got up early and hid it again on the bookcase.  Only this time, inside the box containing the balsawood Fokker biplane model Jeff and I were going to build when he was 9. It's been sitting there for the last 13 years, no matter where I've moved. We'll get around to building it one day. Probably, I suspect, during one spur-of-the-moment night under the inspiration of a couple of six-packs.

That night I found the angel sitting in the cockpit of the new red biplane parked just inside my front door.

This, of course, meant war.

For the next week it was carnage. It was also a losing battle. I thought I had her when I hid it in the toe of the suit of armor, but my depression only deepened when I found it swinging gently from the pommel of the sword.

She was starting to toy with me.

And then one morning, just as I ... 1. Was nearing my wits end; 2. Had filled near to bursting; 3. Had had it up to here; 4. All of the above (hint: pick 4), it came to me. The perfect solution. The ideal hiding place. A place where she would never find that angel in a million years!

And most important, it would mean the end of this stupid game.

The next morning I stepped forth into the dawn, filled with new-found confidence, my head tipped at a jaunty angle and a smug smile on my lips. Tucking a bit of wisteria in my lapel, I knew I had her.

The living room was dark and foreboding as I eased open the front door. Looking down, I knew why. There was no angel.

Isis was feigning sleep on the couch, but I could see her ears were flattened tight against her head, a sure sign of her pent-up rage.

"Nobody likes a sore loser," I grinned.

She raised one side of her mouth in a sneer and hissed loudly.

I whistled loudly into the kitchen to treat myself to something cold and thirst-quenching and celebrate my hard-won victory. I patted the tiny bulge in my pocket with satisfaction, pleased at the little edge in knowledge I had gained through this experience.

If you're going to beat a Siamese ... you have to cheat.

There's something in the patio

My slobbery Siamese licked me awake in the pre-dawn darkness of yesterday morning.

I think I opened my eyes. It's hard to tell when it's just as dark with them open as it is with them closed.

"Merr!" Isis said. *Something's in the patio.*

"So what?" growled the Papa bear. "Somebody's been sleeping in my bed, and he'd like to be doing it again."

"Merr!" she repeated, taking hold of my nose gently in her fangs. *Please come look?*

Siamese cats can be most persuasive.

I rolled off the waterbed and stared into the rug for awhile and then staggered to my feet, kicking the edge of the book case with my big toe, and hopped the rest of the way into the living room, slamming my elbow against the metal wall heater with a loud BANG, and stepped on the cat with a loud MERROW! as we reached the sliding door to the patio.

If there was anything left in the patio it had to be deaf, dumb, or bigger than a refrigerator.

As I knelt down to unfasten the cat's mouth from my ankle, I stared out into the patio, waiting for my eyes to become accustomed to the darkness. I always leave the door open with just the screen closed, so Isis can enjoy the night.

A sudden rustle of leaves over in the corner caught our attention.

I was on my hands and knees and Isis was suddenly underneath me, peering out between my arms.

"Coward," I whispered. "I thought you were supposed to guard the house?"

A large white blur suddenly scurried across the patio and climbed on top of some cardboard boxes next to the fence.

A big ... uh, make that HUGE lab rat? I was suddenly awake. This was getting interesting.

No, it was a white opossum! From the size of it, about three months old. There's a strain of white opossums that occurs spottily throughout the San Francisco Bay Area. They're not albinos, usually having dark eyes, ears and occasionally dark feet that looks like they're wearing shoes.

Isis and I crouched there quietly watching our visitor as it methodically sniffed its way through the empty boxes in search of things to nibble on. It stopped twice to munch on something, making loud, smacking sounds with it's enormous mouth. Probably a cricket or a spider.

Opossums are omnivorous and will eat, literally, anything. I suspect they could survive on dried grass if they had to. But with all the free catfood they find on our back doorsteps, I doubt that theory will ever be tested.

No wonder all my banging around hadn't bothered the little prowler. Opossums are not very bright, their brainwaves devoted primarily to sniffing out prey, so they hunt with a single-minded focus that would do credit to a professional poker player

Actually that sort of intensity is important to a young opossum's survival.

Most wild mammals at that age would still be under the tutelage of their mama, but with opossums it's different. They come from a large family, six to eight, and as they grow in size and spill out of the mother's pouch, they transfer to her back. There they hang on for dear life with mouthfuls, handfuls and prehensiletailfuls of fur until they eventually get dislodged.

From that point on those little guys are on their own. It's a big world out there, full of owls and dogs and curious cats, but opossums have somehow managed to proliferate and become one of our most common local mammals.

As we watched, the youngster worked its way around the perimeter of the patio until it was just on the other side of the screen.

"HISS!" snapped Isis, lunging forward for effect. *Get out of my face!*

"HISS!" responded the opossum, crashing wildly off through the dry leaves and into the night. *I'm going already!*

As I've said before, it's a wacky little household I've got here, but hey, I kinda like it.

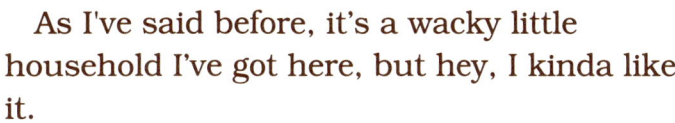

"Can we go back to bed now?"